The Secret Friend

For Stephen Fry
J. D.

For Philippa, who likes letters
H. C.

Text copyright © 1999 by Joyce Dunbar
Illustrations copyright © 1999 by Helen Craig

First U.S. edition 1999

Library of Congress Cataloging-in-Publication Data

Dunbar, Joyce.
The secret friend / Joyce Dunbar ; illustrated by Helen Craig.—1st U.S. ed.
p.   cm.—(Panda and Gander stories)
Summary: Panda feels a little hurt after helping his best friend Gander write a
letter to Gander's secret friend.
ISBN 0-7636-0720-7
[1. Best friends—Fiction. 2. Letter writing—Fiction. 3. Geese—Fiction.
4. Pandas—Fiction.] I. Craig, Helen, ill. II. Title. III. Series: Dunbar, Joyce.
Panda and Gander stories
PZ7.D8944Sd   1998
[E]—dc21   98-14048*

10 9 8 7 6 5 4 3 2 1

Printed in Hong Kong

This book was typeset in AT Arta.
The pictures were done in watercolor and line.

Candlewick Press
2067 Massachusetts Avenue
Cambridge, Massachusetts 02140

The Secret
Friend

▪▪▪▪▪▪▪▪▪▪▪▪▪▪▪▪▪▪▪▪▪

Joyce Dunbar

illustrated by

Helen Craig

CANDLEWICK PRESS
CAMBRIDGE, MASSACHUSETTS

Today I am going to write a thank-you letter," said Gander.

"Who to?" asked Panda.

"My friend," said Gander.

"Which friend?" asked Panda.

"My secret friend," said Gander.

"I didn't know you had a secret

friend," said Panda.

"Well, I have," said Gander,

"for a while."

"What are you going to thank your secret friend for?" asked Panda.

"I don't know yet," said Gander.

Gander started to write.

Dear secret friend,

Thank-you for—

and then he stopped.

He needed to think about it.

He sat at his desk — and thought.

He sharpened his pencil — and

thought some more.

He went for a walk and thought
all the thoughts he could think of.
Then he had an idea.

Dear secret friend,

Thank-you for

being my friend.

Gander

"There, I have finished my letter,"

he said to Panda.

"Is that it?" asked Panda.

"Yes," said Gander, "that's it."

"Your secret friend won't like it,"
said Panda.

"Why not?" asked Gander.

"Because you haven't finished it
correctly. You've just put 'Gander.'
'Gander' isn't enough."

"What should I put?" asked Gander.

"That depends," said Panda.

"On what?" asked Gander.

"How much you care about your secret friend," said Panda.

"A lot," said Gander.

"Well, maybe you should put 'Best wishes, Gander.'"

"Oh, I care about him more than that," said Gander.

"You do?" said Panda.

"I do," said Gander.

"Then you could put

'Love, Gander,'" said Panda.

So Gander put

"Love, Gander."

"Or you could put

'Lots of love, Gander,'" said Panda.

So Gander crossed out

"Love, Gander" and put

"Lots of love, Gander."

"Or you could put

'Lots and lots of love, Gander,'"

said Panda.

So Gander put "Lots and"

in front of "Lots of love,

Gander."

Dear secret friend,
Thank you for
being my friend.
~~Love, Gander~~
Lots and lots of love,
Gander

"What else could I put?"

asked Gander.

"Three kisses," said Panda.

So Gander put three kisses.

"And a big red heart," said Panda.

So Gander put a big red heart.

"Now that's enough," said Panda.

"I think I will stick some stickers
on it as well," said Gander.
He stuck on a star sticker and
a dinosaur sticker and a monster
sticker and a spaceship sticker.
"That's enough stuff," said Panda.

"I think I will draw a picture as well
and put a pattern all around the
edge," said Gander.

And Gander drew a duck holding
a bunch of balloons and made
a pattern all around the edges.

"There," he said when he had finished.

"Now I think that's enough.

Now I can send my letter."

"To your secret friend," said Panda.

"That's right," answered Gander.

"And your secret friend might answer

your letter," said Panda.

"That's right."

"Or he might not," said Panda.

"I'm sure he will," said Gander.

"But he might not put a

row of kisses," said Panda.

"He might not draw a big red heart.

He might not put stickers or

do a drawing or make a pattern.

He might not even put 'Lots and

lots of love.' He might just put

'Your secret friend.'"

"Well, I will send it all the same,"

said Gander.

"See if I care," said Panda.

Gander went to mail his letter.

He made a slot in a shoebox and

put the letter in the slot. Then he

went back to see Panda.

Panda was sitting and pouting.

"What's the matter, Panda?"

asked Gander.

Panda just pouted.

"A letter arrived in

the mailbox.

Do you want to

see who it's for?"

Panda just kept

pouting.

"I'll go and see," said Gander.

Gander opened the mailbox and

took out the letter.

"Well, well, well!" he said.

"This looks like the one I just mailed!

It didn't take long to arrive.

Look what it says on the envelope—

'TO MY DEAR

SECRET FRIEND,

PANDA!'"